Andrea Beck

Goodnight, Canada

North Winds Press
An Imprint of Scholastic Canada Ltd.

The illustrations for this book were created using pencil crayon and paint on coloured paper.

Library and Archives Canada Cataloguing in Publication

Beck, Andrea, 1956-
Goodnight, Canada / by Andrea Beck.

ISBN 978-1-4431-0782-2

I. Title.

PS8553.E2948G66 2012   jC813'.54   C2012-901662-4

6 5 4 3 2 1   Printed in Malaysia 46   12 13 14 15 16

To you, wherever you may be.
– A. B.

I'm in bed in my house,
   where the land meets the sea.
If I sit at my window,
   will you look for me?

Where are you out there?
Are you off to bed too?
Then goodnight to me,
    and goodnight to you.
Goodnight to us,
    and Canada too.

Goodnight to the provinces, sea to sea.
Goodnight to the territories, one, two, three.
We'll follow the dusk from east to west,
    and up to the north to tuck in the rest.

And so . . .
Goodnight, Newfoundland and Labrador.

Goodnight, Nova Scotia.

Goodnight,
Prince Edward Island.

Goodnight, New Brunswick.

Goodnight, Quebec.
Bonne nuit.

Goodnight, Ontario.

Goodnight, Manitoba.

Goodnight, Saskatchewan.

Goodnight, Alberta.

Goodnight, British Columbia.

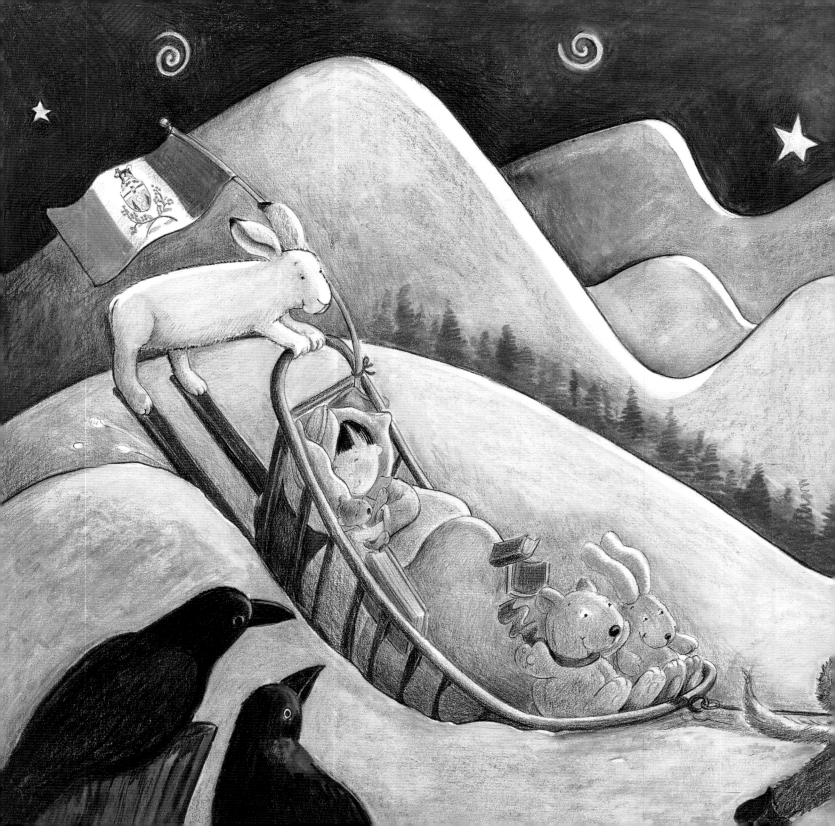

And up to Yukon, goodnight.

Goodnight,
Northwest Territories.

Goodnight,
Nunavut.

And goodnight,
world.